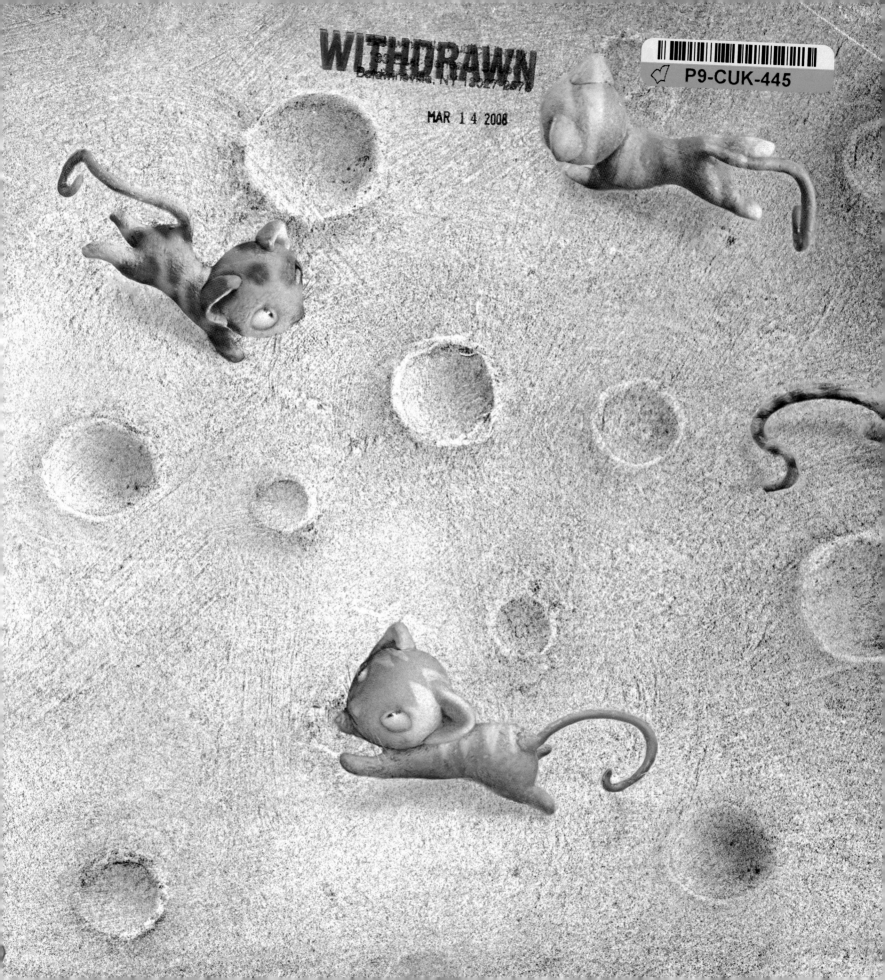

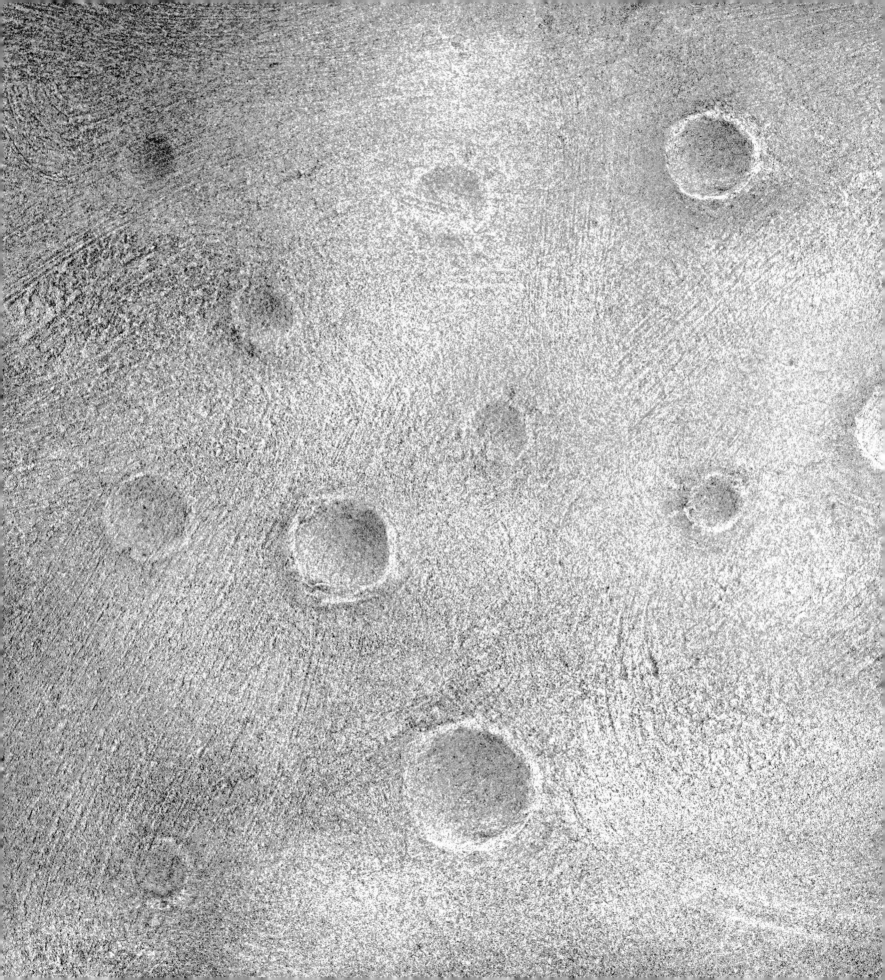

Oscar and the Mooncats

*For Dayhunter and Wallace, one on the earth
and one on the moon.*
—L.G.R.

For Davide and Maura—thank you!
—N.C.

www.houghtonmifflinbooks.com

The text of this book is set in ITC Golden Cockerel .
The illustrations are done in mixed media, including plasticine, acrylics, collage, and computer graphics.
Book design by Carol Goldenberg

Library of Congress Cataloging-in-Publication Data

Rymond, Lynda Gene.
Oscar and the mooncats / by Lynda Gene Rymond ; illustrated by Nicoletta Ceccoli.
p. cm.
Summary: Feeling more than a little wild, Oscar the cat leaps from one high spot to
another until he lands on the Moon, where he plays with the mooncats until his boy
begins to call and he must find a way back home or risk becoming a mooncat, himself.
ISBN-13: 978-0-618-56316-6 (hardcover)
ISBN-10: 0-618-56316-4 (hardcover)
[1. Cats—Fiction. 2. Moon—Fiction. 3. Adventure and adventurers—Fiction.]
I. Ceccoli, Nicoletta, ill. II. Title.
PZ7.R984Osc 2007
[E]—dc22
2006026079
Printed in Singapore
TWP 10 9 8 7 6 5 4 3 2 1

Oscar
and the
Mooncats

by Lynda Gene Rymond
illustrated by Nicoletta Ceccoli

HOUGHTON MIFFLIN COMPANY · BOSTON 2007

O scar loved his boy.

He also loved stinky cat food for breakfast and crunchy cat food for dinner. He loved his catnip mouse and his red pillow by the window.

More than anything else, though, he loved to jump up to places where he could watch . . . *everything*.

One evening, while his boy helped with the dishes, Oscar hopped up on a chair, then to the table, and from there to the top of the refrigerator.

"Come down before you get into trouble," said his boy.

But the tall bookcase in the living room was just a leap or two away. So Oscar jumped from the fridge to the chandelier, and from the chandelier to the top of the bookcase. He blinked at his boy, who scolded, "Oscar, you're wild tonight. Come down!"

Oscar *was* feeling wild. When his boy went in for a bath, Oscar leapt from the bookcase to the windowsill, out the window to a tree, and from the tree to the very peak of the garage.

Wow! thought Oscar. *Look at it all!* Oscar could see his boy in the bubble bath, the hop-toads in the lettuce patch, the bumblebees in the roses. He could see the awful dog-thing next door. Oscar could see up the street . . . a little way. He could see down the street . . . a little way.

Then Oscar saw the crescent moon rising over town, its tip hanging just low enough. He wriggled back on his haunches, sprang into the mightiest leap of his life . . .

. . . and landed in a cloud of moon dust.

"Meow! Meow!" Sliding down the slope of the moon were two of the biggest cats Oscar had ever seen.

"Who are you?" asked Oscar, a little frightened.

"Why, we're mooncats! Who are *you*?"

"I'm Oscar. I'm an earthcat."

The mooncats looked at each other and smiled.

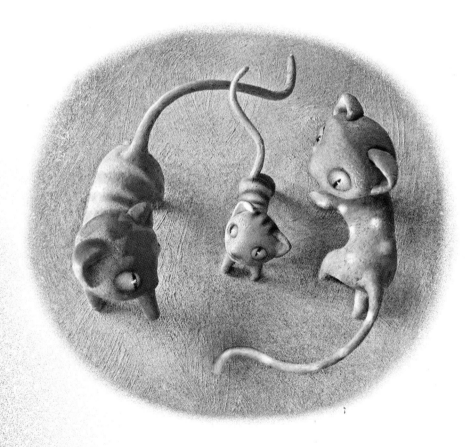

"Do you like to play?" they asked.

"Of course!" he answered.

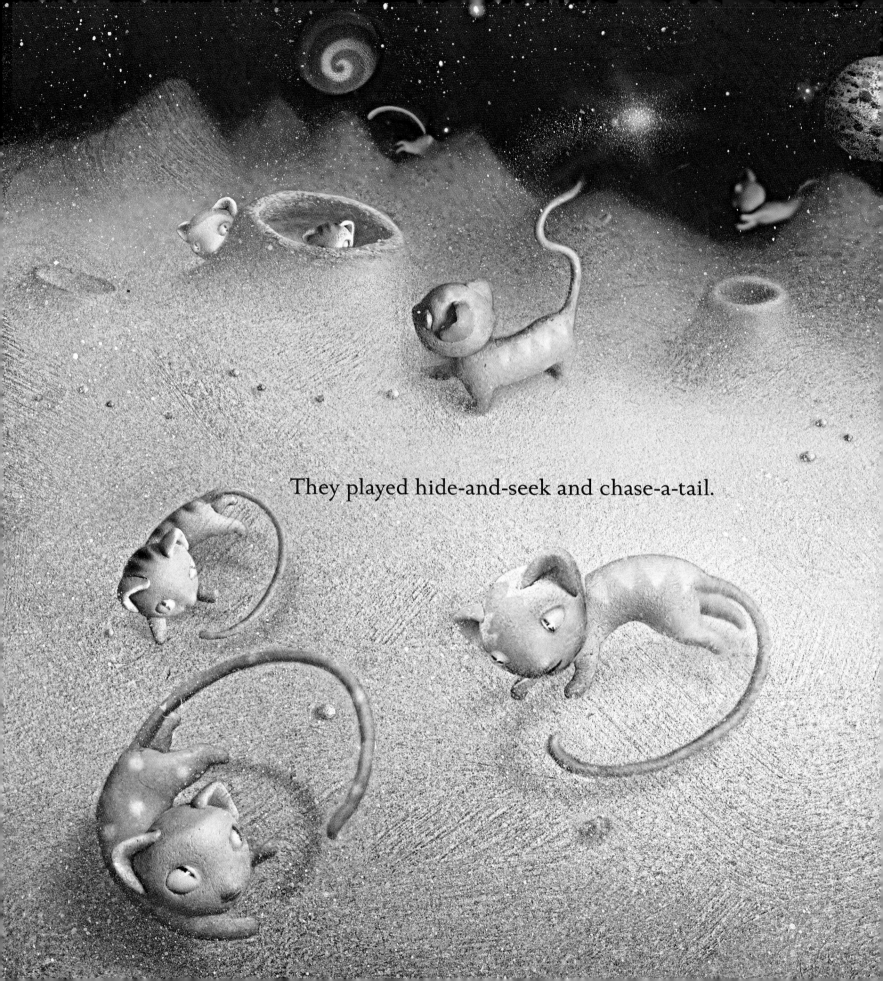

They played hide-and-seek and chase-a-tail.

They played pounce-on-the-moon-mountain

and pretend-there's-a-mouse.

They played until Oscar flopped on
his side, panting.

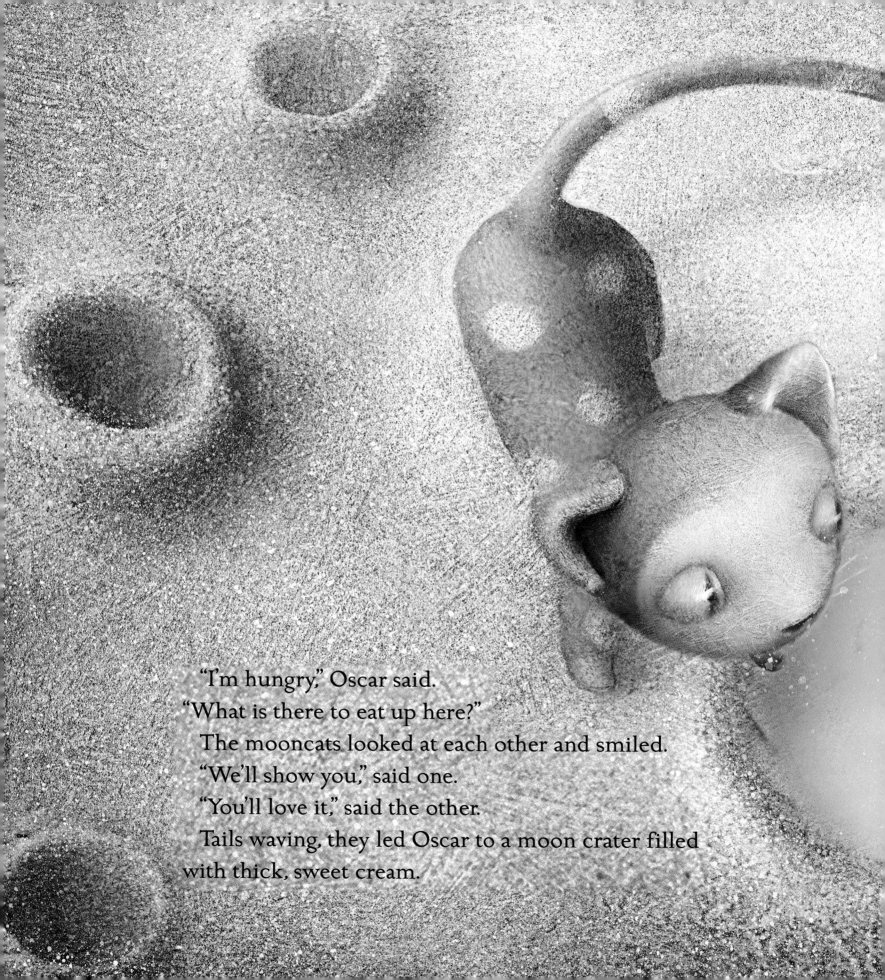

"I'm hungry," Oscar said.
"What is there to eat up here?"
  The mooncats looked at each other and smiled.
  "We'll show you," said one.
  "You'll love it," said the other.
  Tails waving, they led Oscar to a moon crater filled
with thick, sweet cream.

"Where does this come from?" asked Oscar.

"There's a cow who jumps over the moon," said the mooncats. "She leaves it for us."

Oscar bent his head to drink, but before he could take a sip, he heard something. It was faint but clear.

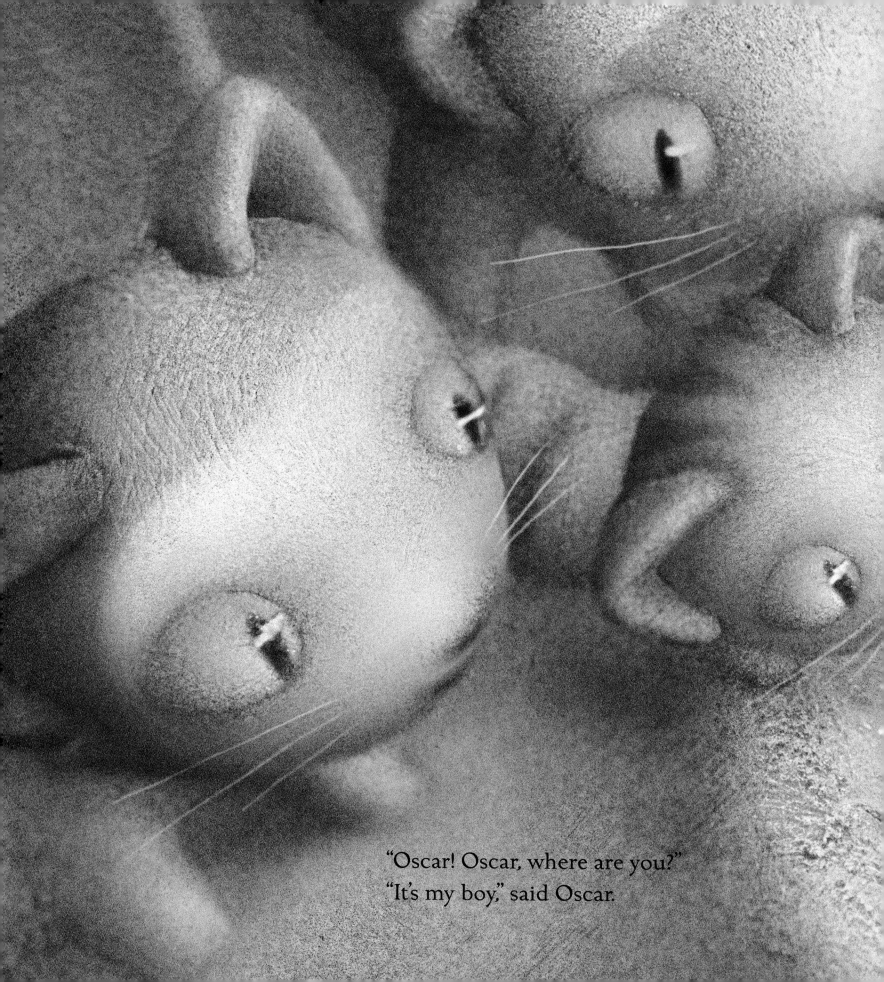

"Oscar! Oscar, where are you?"
"It's my boy," said Oscar.

"What's a boy?" asked one mooncat.

"Have a drink," said the other.

"I am awfully thirsty," said Oscar. "Just a quick drink, and then I'll go." He put out his tongue to taste —

"Oscar! Come home, Oscar."

"There he is again," said Oscar.

"I don't hear anything," said one mooncat.

"Have a drink," said the other.

"Right," said Oscar. He bent to drink.

"DON'T!" shouted a deep voice. Oscar
looked up into the face of a big spotted
cow. "Bad mooncats! Shoo! Scat!" The
cow lowered her nose to Oscar's face
and gently breathed in. "I *thought* I
smelled an earthcat."

"Why did you scare my friends away?"
asked Oscar. His tiger fur stood on end.

"Are they your friends?" replied the cow. "Those mooncats jumped here so long ago, they've forgotten their people. And I'm no earthcow. If you drink this cream, your coat will grow pale and shine like silver, and your eyes will glow with the pearly moonlight. Your boy would never know you again."

"Come home, come home, Oscar!"

"That's my boy," said Oscar.

Oscar ran to the edge of the moon. "The moon is much higher now! Look, there is the city, and there is the countryside, and there is my town right between. There is the highway and the river. There is the street where I live, there is my house, and I can even see my boy. How will I ever get home?"

"It's too far away, even for a jumping cat like you," agreed the cow. "I suppose you might as well drink some cream after all, and go play with the mooncats."

"What about my boy?"

"He'll forget you in time," sighed the cow. "And you, him. Good luck."

The cow gathered herself and vaulted into the starry sky.
But something very quick and tiger-striped sprang onto
her back and clung for dear life.

"What are you doing?" bellowed the cow.

"That's not true," yelled Oscar. "My boy would *never* forget me!"

"Oh, little one," said the cow. "I don't head back to earth. For me, it's Venus and beyond."

"Then goodbye," said Oscar, and he let go. He tumbled
through the night sky, twisting and falling as cats do, his paws
outstretched, his claws at the ready. Oscar fell and fell, but he
thought of his boy and looked for home.

"There," he whispered, "there is the river, and there is our
town. There is our street, and there's the roof—I can make it!"

Oscar landed with an awful bump, but he just shook himself and stretched. He smiled, thinking, *I may not be the first cat to jump up to the moon, but I bet I'm the first cat to jump back down.* He scampered from the roof and ran to the porch, where his boy stood in pajamas, waiting.

"There you are! Where on earth did you go?"

Oscar blinked as if he hadn't been gone at all and led the way to the kitchen, where his boy poured a bowl of crunchy cat food and sat stroking Oscar until every morsel was gone.

Then his boy led the way down the hall, and Oscar made one last jump—onto the bed. He washed the moon dust off his paws and curled up tight.

"Good night, wild Oscar," said his boy. "I wish I knew where you ran off to."

But Oscar was already asleep, dreaming of his next big leap—and of always, *always* coming home.

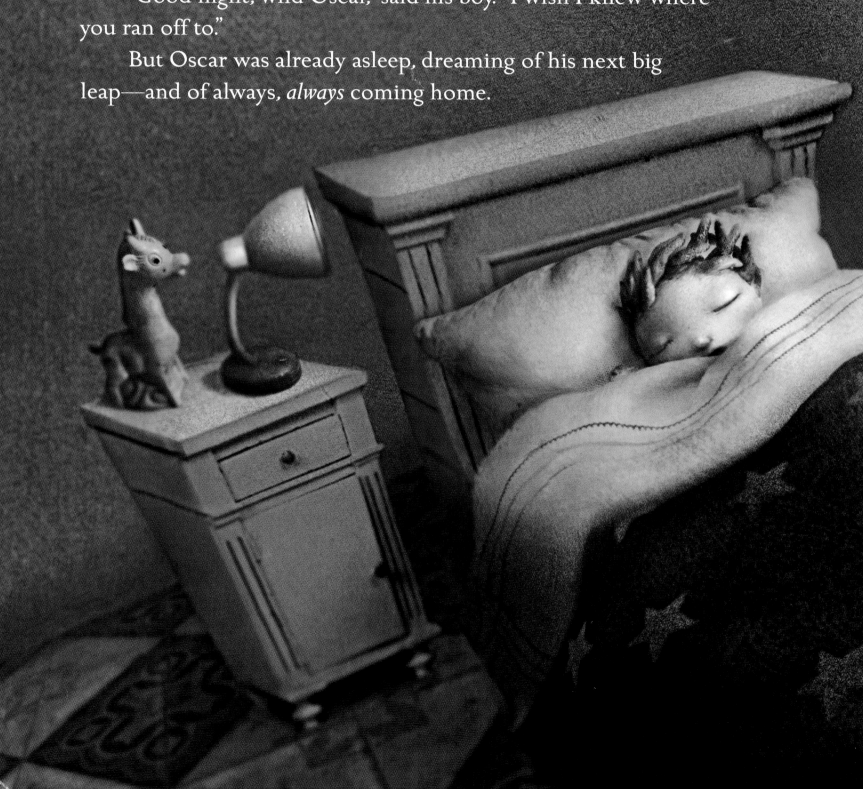

The End

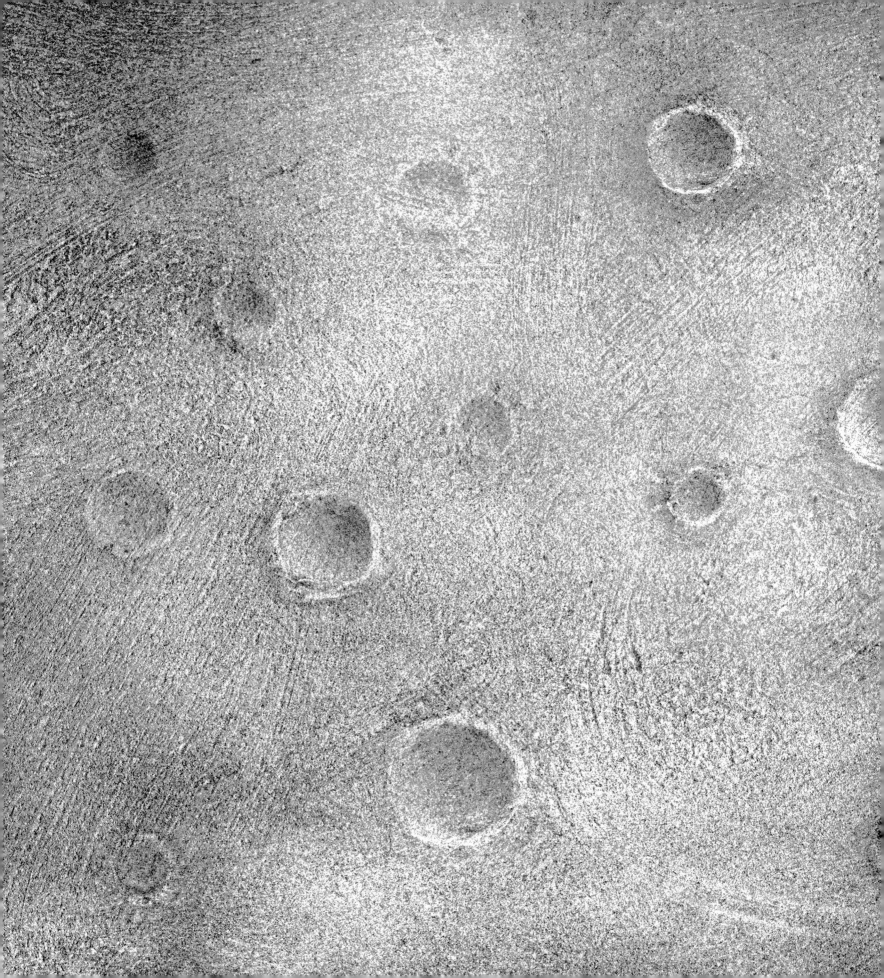

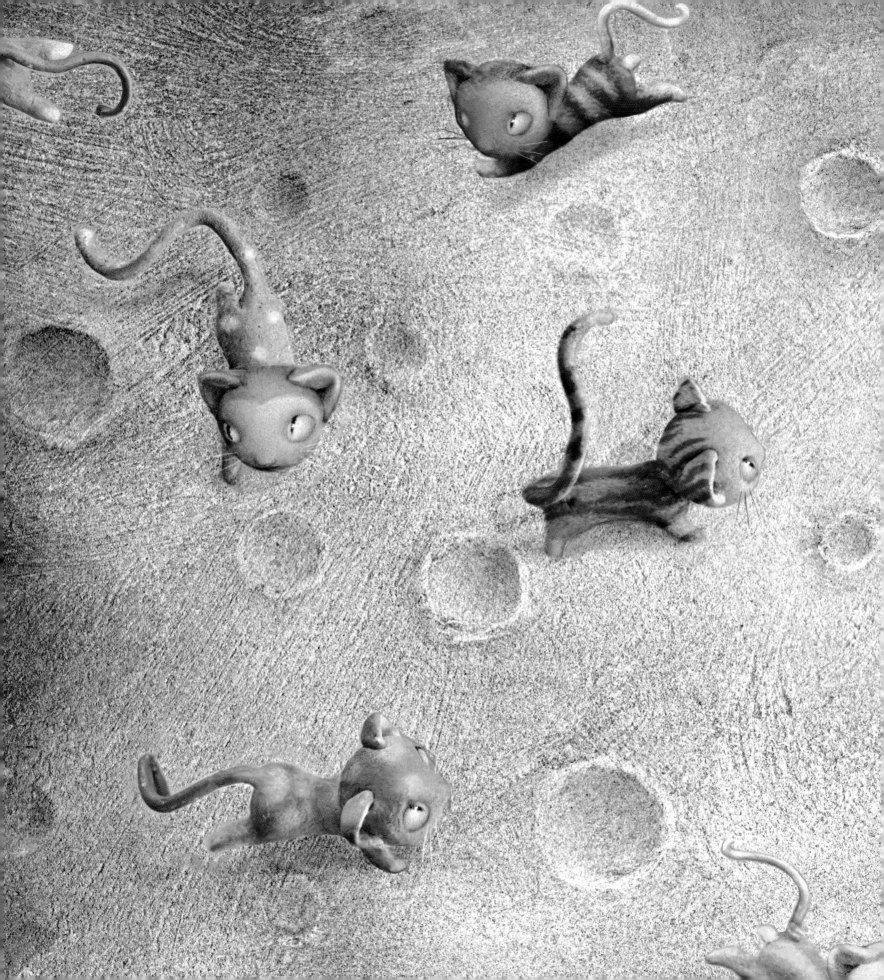